The Paraffin Lamp

The Paraffin Lamp

Kathleen Blanchfield

RECTORY PRESS

Published by
Rectory Press
Portlaw, Co. Waterford, Ireland

ISBN No: 1-903698-08-1

for my husband Michael,
and our daughters
Denise, Marie, Caroline, and Michelle

PATRONS
Winfield Construction, Clone
First Active, Kilkenny
St. Canice's Credit Union, Kilkenny
O'Shea's Super Valu, Ballyraggett
The Kilkenny People
AIB, High Street, Kilkenny

Part of the Proceeds from the Sale of this Book will go
to Cancer Research

Acknowledgements:
Thanks are due to the editors of the following publica-
tions in which some of these poems first appeared:
Kilkenny People, Tipperary Star,
SMA Magazine, Radio Kilkenny,
and Poetry Today (UK).

The author wishes to thank Edward Power for his edito-
rial expertise; Joseph Woods (Director, Poetry Ireland)
for his encouragement and support. A special thanks to
my husband, Michael, and the family, for just being there.

CONTENTS

Our Own Seasons

Our childhood is life's springtime
When all the world is young;
We love all of the childhood things
And have such joy and fun.

Our adulthood is summertime,
We grow towards that freedom;
We taste the fruits of life's sweet wine
And live it's joyful season.

Our middle years bring autumn time –
The harvest of our lives;
And in this rust & amber time
Contentment glows and shines.

Our senior years, life's wintertime,
Bring wisdom to the soul;
We pray God grants us peace of mind
And the key to realms of gold.

My Little Field Of Dreams

Sometimes I see a little field
In a valley in my dreams,
The greenest, freshest little field,
So peaceful and serene.

Its trees are filled with ripened fruit,
And snow white roses grow,
Butterflies float gently through it
And sunlit waters flow.

The melodies of song birds
Would lift the saddest heart
To moments far above mere words,
Beyond all earthly art.

I see no people there at all,
But sense great love around
Entwined with peace and perfect joy,
And happiness profound.

In my little field of dreams
I want to lay my care,
And sleep that sleep forever
In its peacefulness so rare.

Sweet St. Patrick's Day

Back in the 1950's
On Saint Patrick's Day,
Green badges and green ribbons,
We went along our way,

Donned the tiny shamrock
And walked the road to Mass
Where 'hail glory of Saint Patrick'
Was sung by lad and lass.

Parades in our marble city
Were music-filled I know,
And colourful beyond belief,
A memorable show.

Being too young to understand,
Or admire the drummer boys,
Homeward bound we longed to be
For our very own surprise.

You see, the Lenten fast was on,
But on Saint Patrick's Day
The goodies that we fasted from
Were all put in our way.

We relished then the fruit pastilles,
And fruit gums sweet to chew;
'Lolly Pops' and 'Billiard Balls',
'Peggy's Legs' and 'Bull's Eyes' too.

Slab toffee it was such a treat
And bon-bons were delicious;
And when the lemonade was served
We then had all our wishes.

Alas, Saint Patrick's Day flew by,
The simple pleasures gone;
Next morning we awoke and found
Our Lenten fast back on.

4

Flowers Of May

Like flowing lace the hedges glow
With May's soft petals white;
Wild flowers bloom in glory-cloaks
And summer garlands bright.

For years we placed these blossoms
'Neath a statue in our home,
And a tender prayer we whispered there
To Mary so well known.

No fingers green, no special care,
But nature own sweet way,
Made of the little flowers
So perfect a display.

Their scent was next to heavenly,
Unique was their array;
They're something truly special,
Those sweet wild flowers of May.

Moon Magic

Peeping through my bedroom window,
Friend of all my childhood days,
Soft moonbeams caress my pillow,
Serene and gentle silver haze.

A child back then, an adult now,
I marvel at your sight,
Strolling in your peaceful glow,
Amazing in the night.

Moonlight shadows at close of day,
Misty nights with moonbeams filled,
Secret kisses enhanced by magic,
Romance blossomed, and my heart thrilled.

People of forgotten ages
Were guided by your light,
Escorting them to tend their herds
In deep black winter night.

I pray that man will not destroy
Your serene and radiant sight,
As you caress our war-torn earth
With timeless silver light.

Lisdowney

In a quiet country village
Quaint and picturesque;
We schooled our little children
As they set out on life's quest.

In Larry, Josie and Ailish
We couldn't ask for better
Our little children for to teach,
And get on well together.

To Frank and Annie's grocery shop.
I travelled every day
To pick our little children up
From school just down the way.

Carmel had the friendly pub
Just by the chapel gate,
Where we often had a sample of
Choice drinks of splendid taste.

Nobly stands Lisdowney church
Saint Brigid to behold;
Springtime brings her special touch,
For, then, her story's told.

Lisdowney spans Clontubrid
And scenic Gathabawn,
Where that charming name *as Gaeilge*
Is very proudly known.

The hurling field holds many tales
Of loss and victory,
And many of these sporting teams
Went down in history.

Lisdowney and its countryside
So quaint and picturesque;
Hurling and camogie teams,
And victory and rest.

Country School

Gathering apples
Sweet and sour,
Cracking hazelnuts
Hour on hour

Picking blackberries,
Rose hips too,
In russet hedgerows
'Neath skies of blue

Chestnuts and acorns
Fall from the trees;
It's back-to-school time
September's breeze

Good-bye to you, Mum,
And Dad now farewell.
Back at my school
This great story I'll tell.

time

like a great
one-way ship
sails onward
takes the world
on board
no first class
no distinctions
no reservations
no returns
no waiting
just time and tide
seeing all
to journey's end

The Broken Rose

Alone in my sun-kissed garden
I welcomed the summer's first rose;
But my little dog playful beside me
Shattered its enchanting pose.

Just like a limb that's been broken,
It hung as if crying for care,
So I placed a support all around it,
And said this little prayer:

Please, Lord, protect your creation
In the very first day of its bloom;
Strengthen its tiny frail stem, Lord,
And bring it to beauty then soon.

Next morning I strolled in my garden
And could scarcely believe my own eyes,
The little rose stood O so elegantly
And wafted its scent to the skies.

And I was glad I was able
To help it grow right fair;
For like all of us it needed,
Some tender loving care.

My Kilkenny

Medieval city
Majestic by the Nore,
Your noble castle stands
Amid stories of yore.

When the great ocean beckoned
We drifted away,
Still you lingered in mind
Till we came back one day

To this home place remembered,
For sweet childhood things,
For fun and for laughter,
And young teenage dreams.

For the Mayfair and Carlton,
To see showbands new,
The Savoy and the Regent,
The pictures to view.

Now ballrooms have vanished,
Night Clubs take their place,
And Cineplex now
Is the all-new film base.

Still, amidst all this progress,
Some special thoughts fly
To my youth in Kilkenny
And days now gone by.

Omagh

The sun shines bright in Omagh,
Sometimes they wonder why,
For deep in troubled hearts
Darkened chambers lie.

O let us all remember
Omagh's darkest day,
And on its anniversary
For Omagh let us pray.

Kilkenny joins you silently
In reflection on this day,
In city and in country,
We're with you as we pray.

May God take home the Omagh dead,
And the injured's health restore;
And to those who lost their loved ones
Bring solace evermore.

O let us all remember
In August as we pray
And keep its anniversary,
Brave Omagh's darkest day.

I Feel Your Presence

I feel your presence near me, Lord.
Someday I'll see your face,
When from this world you call me home
To heaven's own eternal place.

You struggled the hill of Calvary,
They nailed you to the Cross,
But they didn't realise their deed
Would be their greatest loss.

As your life so cruelly ebbed away,
You cried out with great thirst.
But they ignored your painful cry
And put their harsh ways first.

As I wander through this troubled world,
Within my heart I place
The sorrows and the suffering
You endured to save our race.

I feel your presence near me, Lord,
This makes me stand life's pace;
I'll walk with you until the end,
And then feel your embrace.

14

Love and Crosses

In a springtime garden
Two people met one day
And admired the tiny wild flowers
Peeping through the wintered clay.

They spoke about the springtime
And the golden daffodil;
They watched the little wild birds
As they walked beside the rill.

They looked at one another
And saw God's love shine through;
Their friendship was so pure of heart,
Bestowed upon a few.

She spoke about the crosses,
And he of love so fine;
These were, of course, St. Brigid
And our sweet Valentine.

Valentine's Day

On this special day
St. Valentine's
The day of romance
May you experience
No matter who
You are
No matter where
The joy of holding hands
The comfort of a caring kiss
The warmth of a loving
Arm around you
The pleasure of a smile
The gentle whisper of
tender romantic words
And may all these things
Together
Costing nothing
Lead you to the garden
Of truelove
Where, even through
The bad times,
The blossoms will stay
Forever in bloom.

Blessed Mother Theresa

Blessed Mother Theresa
Unselfish and sharing
Essence of loving
And core of all caring

Spiritual, kind,
Faith all undaunted;
Worldly riches
You never wanted.

Humble, sincere,
Thoughtful and true;
These words just begin
To tell about you.

In Glendalough

Snowdrops bunch
'Neath ancient walls,
A tiny robin sings
In the breeze.

Among St. Kevin's headstones -
The names of those long gone -
I feel the sacred stillness,
The wisdom of this place.

St. Theresa's Reliquary

In my childhood I remember
St. Theresa's picture frame:
A little old and worn, perhaps,
But in it still remained

A face so young and beautiful,
Glowing childlike innocence;
For her I learned and kept
Great love and reverence.

Here am I now, decades later,
Having seen her reliquary,
Where I felt a special stillness,
Peace and tranquility.

I saw the great clouds gather
One cold April afternoon,
When people came together
Midst Celtic Tiger boom

Took time to contemplate awhile
On Theresa's life so dear,
To linger and to venerate
This saint of yesteryear.

Took time from our own restlessness,
And from our turbulent world,
To kneel, to pray, and dwell upon
This little flower's words.

This shows that we are reaching out,
And longing deep within
For something more than worldly things,
For God's love to dwell herein.

Then when the crowds all drifted,
And her reliquary moved on,
Something warm and special
Stayed with us, every one.

The Cappa Farmhouse

The winding road to Bonnetstown
Leads to a leafy lane
And to the Cappa farmhouse
Where lives my Auntie May.

Brother Jim and I were happy
To leave all else aside
And walk right down to Cappa
During school holiday time.

We played with our first cousins
Just a mile or two from home;
And through the fields of blossoms
How happily we did roam.

Down to Uncle Martin's, then,
Who to the Creamery went;
And on the river's hazel bank
Many happy hours we spent.

The aroma of May's baking
Lingered in the air;
O there was no mistaking
Her bread beyond compare.

Then in the shadow of the night
Time for prayer was found,
The Rosary we'd all recite
Together kneeling down.

Now mem'ries dwell in older hearts,
Imprinted on our minds;
We never from our childhoods part
Through all the changing times.

No Time

No time to stop in this world
No time to stare awhile
At the beauty of the budding rose
Or the warmth of a smile.

No time to watch the summer skies
Or rainbow's pretty hue,
No time to stop and listen
To the pigeon's husky coo.

No time to linger silently
And view the stars at night,
No time to stroll on moonlit strands
And watch the ocean's might.

No time to gaze at meadows
Swaying in the summer breeze,
No time to quietly listen
To the gently rustling breeze.

No time to linger wistfully
At soil so neatly planted;
No time for God's own beauty,
All's taken now for granted.

No time.
No time.
No time.

The Holly Tree In Ballykeefe

There's a holly tree in Ballykeefe
Where Mam and Dad now lie,
And by their grave in disbelief
Sometimes I question why.

Their lives and hardship were entwined
And they only lived to see
A fraction of the better times
Enjoyed by you and me.

Then feelings overwhelmed me,
My thoughts ran very free,
And I questioned God in Ballykeefe
Beneath the holly tree:

'Why did you take them from this world
Before we could repay
Some of the comfort they deserved
After the livelong day?'

Then a gentle force engulfed me
And whispered 'Humankind,
With intellect and will so weak,
Why question power divine?'

All questions then were brushed aside
By a soothing summer breeze,
And I knew that God was on my side
By the grave in Ballykeefe.

At Home In Patrick Street

As I stroll through tranquil Patrick Street
And think of times gone past,
I dwell on those unhurried days
That were not long to last.

I picture Dick with fishing rods
By the banks of the great Nore,
I remember the kingfishers
With colours blue and gold.

I picture Molly in her chair
Awaiting Dick's return,
Dear Molly, she was always there
To make the house a home.

They had no children of their own
I loved their company;
It was to me a second home
A welcome place to be.

There was a sense of homeliness
At number eighty-six,
Their home was such a cosy place,
In peaceful Patrick Street.

Alas their house is there no more
And both of them have gone;
Still, Dick and Molly by the Nore
In memories live on.

The Paraffin Lamp

There you now stand
In proud elegant style,
Just as you stood
When I was a child.

I remember your light
And your soft, gentle glow,
As we struggled with homework
In the sweet long ago.

Down all our years
Your shadowy light,
So soft and so peaceful,
Shone all through the night.

So still in our home,
Though now we've all grown,
There's a snug little spot
That you call your own.

You show off your globe
Each day of the week,
And you glow with the pride
Of a special antique.

You shine your light now
At great family times,
And not just for reading
Those boring school lines.

You shine it at Easter,
Yuletide and New Year,
Transporting us back
To the times we hold dear.

O there you still stand
In proud elegant style,
Just as you did
When I was a child.

Radio Days

The little wooden wireless
With its golden mesh-like front
Was where I first heard melodies,
Speeches, songs and chants.

I loved that little wireless
When I was just a child;
I listened to so many things.
I imagined men inside.

As I grew to teenage years
I was fascinated more
By the lovely Irish music
That made us take the floor.

Then, when I was just eighteen,
A transistor became mine -
A present for my birthday
From a boy I knew so fine.

A great transistor radio
Red and gold and white;
I felt I'd got a fortune
And listened day and night

To Horace Batchelor in praise
Of his 'Station of the Stars';
O, twixt Luxembourg and Eireann
We had news from near and far.

That radio is still my own,
I'm married to the giver;
Michael and the radio -
I'll love them both forever.

My Garden Oak

Noble in your nakedness
Towering o'er my garden,
Winter breezes pierce your limbs,
Shriek fiercely without pardon.

Close by your bare, cold body,
Evergreens swiftly sway;
Charming changes abound
As winter drifts away.

Your denuded frame's then covered
In a handsome coat of green;
When springtime spreads its leafy garb,
You're the finest ever seen.

You umbrella all the roses
And the sweet forget-me-nots,
You protect the little wildflowers
And the tiny household crops.

As I glance at you in summer,
Your beauty's beyond compare;
Standing silently in my garden,
In the fragrant summer air.

The wild birds flock to greet you
And to welcome you when dressed;
The blackbird whistles louder
To show that he's impressed.

Then in autumn's rust and amber
You are like a precious dream;
An enchanting sight so perfect -
My garden oak supreme.

Young Lovers

By the misty seashore
Beneath the evening sky,
Young lovers listened eagerly
To ocean's lullaby.

Summer breezes whispered
Secrets to the sand;
The waves so gently rolled along
As they walked hand in hand.

32

The hazy sunset shadows
Reflected in the sea;
Young lovers walked through paradise
And whispered what could be.

Ballade

The swallows in springtime on Ireland descend,
From far distant places of beauty unknown,
Twittering and swooping at their journey's end,
Till the crisp autumn breezes beckon them home.
These creatures of wonder to the world so well
                                                known,
Never cease to amaze us, their passage well-timed,
In groups they assemble, when home they are
                                                going,
With style and with wisdom and instinct sublime.

Tiny smart builders with ways that enchant us,
Their voyage uniquely fulfilling their quest,
With passion and splendour intrigue and astound
                                                us,
Building and feathering their summertime nest.
A surface of clay softly lined with the best,
perfection of place, the swallows outline,
Protecting tgheir young, they work withy such zest,
With style and with wisdom and instinct sublime.

Swallows now sometimes seek yesteryear's nests,
On arrival all damage repairing,
Shakey foundations, they render and test,
For the next generation preparing.
Their eggs they then lay, with calm and with
                                                caring,
Little chicks hatch with the passing of time;
With great satisfaction they waitfor the rearing,
With style and with wisdom and instinct sublime.

Young swallows appear unfeathered and hungry,
Beautified later with nature so fine;
Already mapped out is their long, distant journey
With style and with wisdom and instinct sublime.

34

Maytime

As Mayday's fragrant morning dawns
And Springtime's left behind,
Summer days are welcomed
And we wish for warmer climes.
The gardens fill with blossoms,
Gentle winds blow from the south.
Mayday whispers summertime
And cuckoo's tune chants out.
Wild birds whistle melodies
Beneath the summer skies;
Swallows drift in Maytime sun,
Bring warmth into our lives.

At Home In Glenfield

When the gorse in golden blossom
Blends with the hawthorn white
Lisdowney's lovely countryside
Welcomes the summer light.

With these enchanting colours
The fresh green fields fulfil
The three shades of our country
By nature's graphic skill.

All around our Glenfield home
'Neath Clontubrid's tranquil hill,
Nature blooms in Maytime
Unspoilt beside the rill.

This Maytime, watch as you pass by
Clontubrid's hedgerows old:
You'll catch a glimpse of Irishness
In green and white and gold.

No poet's craft could equal,
Or painter's art compete,
With these dainty wild creations
And their splendour so complete.

Less of I

Less of I
And more of we,
More of us
And less of me

Would make this world
A better place
For young and old
Of every race.

Enjoy all things,
Ignore all greed,
Share and care
For those in need,

I and me,
You'll be amused,
Two selfish words
Too often used.

Less of I
And more of we,
More of us
And less of me.

Spoken Words

The idle tongue may hurt much more
Than angry clenched fist blow;
Idle gossip cause more pain
Where'er in life we go.

Sorely wounded flesh and bone
In time for sure will heal,
But the hurt that's done by idle tongues
Will fester and congeal.

The kindest heart it will freeze up
And render spirit low,
When anger turns our precious words
On family, friend or foe.

God granted us the gift of speech
And reason to reflect;
Let us make sure our spoken words
Come gentle with respect.

Sonnet For Making Up

Your heart with words I've wounded so unkind.
Words pierced your soul, like flesh the scabbard's
                                                    sword.
What right have I to hurt my wife so fine?
Severe the words that hurt much more than blows.

I'm sorry now and pray that you'll forgive.
Time's here to think and show how much I care
For you, the one for whom each day I live.
Naught now must matter but the love we share.

Stay ever close and tender thoughts entwine.
Too short this life and quarrels are such a waste.
For your sweet charms and fond caress I pine.
My spirit's soothed in your arm embrace.

You are my love, my happiness, my life.
The world's no good without your love, dear wife.

Autumn

Orange, rust and amber,
Autumn's golden glow,
Season to gather
The crops that we sow.

Blackberries and apples
And hazelnuts brown,
In autumn for picking,
Our trees laden down.

40

Fields that are golden
With straw at its best,
And grain that is gathered
With ardour and zest.

A season to thank thee,
Good Lord, first hand,
For food in abundance
In our beautiful land.

Michael Cherry

Wild as the west wind
That in winter blows,
My nephew Michael –
Michael Cherry so bold.

In springtime he loved
To drive far away,
And in summer sun
Made the best of each day.

His passion was hazelnuts.
He picked lots in September,
And enjoyed all the parties
In festive December.

Friends and family, we miss him
And we always will;
There's an emptiness here
That no one else can fill.

A song and a dance
Was his in all seasons,
And I oft-times ponder
On fate and the reason

Michael Cherry's young life
Was lost in its prime,
At aged twenty- five
In a warm autumn time.

My Sister Anne

I was only four years old
And my sister Anne eleven
When she was taken from the fold
To the pastures of sweet heaven.

My parents' hearts were broken.
I was too young to know
Why such sad words were spoken
So many years ago.

For Mam and Dad felt hopelessness
Each time they called her name;
There's still a certain loneliness
That I cannot explain.

As I kneel now by her graveside
In the quiet cemetery,
I ponder on dear Anne's short life
And the things that could not be.

Deep within I miss her,
I wish she had not died:
O Anne, my only sister,
Fond thoughts of you abide.

A Dying Mother's Lament

What will you do when I'm beneath the clay?
Your father now, one year gone to his rest,
No siblings here to comfort you this day,
Child so alone, my special one, God-blessed.

Food and comfort you'll surely have,
And money will be anything but scarce;
But who'll be here, my child, to give you love?
Your need for love my passing won't erase.

My eyes grow tired and weaker grows each limb,   43
My mind is clear, with you I hate to part;
I long to stay, your special songs to sing,
O gentle child encased within my heart.

Winter Beauty

Through all the dreary winter days
There's beauty to be found,
In the wind that whistle through the trees,
And the snow upon the ground.

There's beauty in the hailstones
And the fog that blinds our view,
In thunderstorm andlightning flash
That we have all lived through.

There's beauty in the falling rain
And the frost that makes us shiver,
For all these things make us aware
Of the presence of a giver.

A Thank You Card

Thank you, Mam and Dad for bringing me
Safely into this world;
For eyes that see
And ears that hear,
And limbs that work perfectly.

Thank you both for my childhood years,
For being there
And for just being you.
There are no words to describe
How much you meant to me.

Day's End

Now before I close these pages
Just as I close my day,
For Catherine and John, my parents,
And my sister Anne, I pray.

For Oliver, my Dad-in-Law,
And Mother-in-law Ellen,
May they with their infant daughter
Be united now in heaven.

For all in this book I've mentioned
Who have parted from this world,
It is always my intention
In my heart to fondly hold.

Four Songs

Touched By Eternity

Part of me, yes part of me,
Call it spirit, soul or destiny,
Yes something that's instilled in me,
Drifts from my being, to somewhere free.

chorus
Like summer breezes on the sea,
Feelings that are pure and free,
Engulf me in serenity,
Touching on eternity.

Desires dissolving worldly things,
Happiness and peace it brings,
Thoughts of joy, my mind imprints,
Embraced by angels' gentle wings.

chorus:

A sense of soul, I tell myself,
And thank the Lord for feelings felt.
It's naught to do with world or wealth,
This joyfulness so kindly dealt.

chorus:

I really think it's that of love,
Deep within, but from above,
Sent here assuring God's own love,
On wings divine, He interwove.

chorus
Like summer breezes on the sea,
Feelings that are pure and free,
Engulf me in serenity,
Touching on eternity.

Recorded by Phil Summers

Shattered Dreams

On the eleventh of September
Two thousand and one,
With regret we remember
The evil deeds done,
When without any warning
A nation so free
On a mid-autumn morning
Faced inhumanity.

chorus:
God bless America,
Keep watch from above.
God bless America,
Show your tender love.
Soothe the bereaved with your solace,
bathye the injured with care,
And to those taken from us,
Let heaven be theirs.

Shattered lived, shattered dreams,
paralysing the world,
When hatred wove reams
Of acts so absurd.
Tears in their torrents,
Streamed the eyes of the world,
Nothing could warrant
This atrocity, Lord.

chorus:

Dear Lord walk beside them
And light up their way;
With divine power guide them
Each minute of each day.
For in God they all trust
In good times and bad,
They need you , O so much
In their times now so sad.

chorus:

Recorded by Noel Fogarty

First Love

In dreams I see the wildflowers
Down by the river bed;
I can almost sense the fragrance
Of the springtime that we met.
In dreams the river still runs clear
And wildflowers blaze with colour,
The wildbirds sing sweet melodies,
Just like when we were together.

chorus:
First love true and tender,
Why did we have to part?
My first love I'll remember
And keep within my heart.
Circumstances parted us
And forced our separate ways.
The memory of your parting kiss
In my heart forever stays.

These nights we strolled 'neath moonlit skies,
You held your hand in mine.
Something enchanting in your eyes
Captured all of my mind.
In my heart you hold a special place,
You haunt my very soul.
No time or money can erase
The memory of your love.

I've searched for you so many times,
But there's not a single trace;
I'd give the world if I could find
My first love to embrace.
If I could just turn back the years
To that springtime of my dreams,
I'd take my first love in my arms
And live out these memories.

chorus:

Now the bluebells hold their heads so low
Down by that river bed.
The daisies seem to whisper 'O
A great mistake was made'.
The wild birds sing sad melodies
To the lesser celendine.
They grieve beneath the great oak trees
For lost love of yours and mine.

chorus:

Recorded by Noel Fogarty

Peace And Tranquility

On a cold April morning
You came to our shores,
Your presence at dawning
Was hailed and adored.

Your reliquary brought thousands
Down your little way,
Taking time from life's turmoil
To be with you to pray.

chorus:
Theresa of the roses,
Little flower good and true,
Heaven proposes
You saint from Lisieux.
Please bring peace to Ireland
In your gentle way;
Bring peace and tranquility
To our whole world today.

Your relics remind us
Of your life on earth,
While your spirit shines on us
With heavenly mirth.

Intrigued by your innocence
And humility,
I'm now touched by a renaissance
Of serenity.

In countries uneasy
Plant your peaceful rose,
Then, selfless Therese,
Look down as it grows

And blossoms among us
With your tender love;
Then you'll gently promise
Your peace from above.

chorus:

Sung by Tom Bolger